PRAISE

"Mike Maggio's *The Appointment* is a contemporary tale of alienation, bureaucracy, and merciless academia. Maggio's anti-hero tries to seek some help—some human concern for his existential plight—but, like Kafka's K or Tolstoy's dying Ivan Ilych, fails to find the recognition and human warmth he so desperately needs. *The Appointment* is a story of existence and mortality and those who avoid human community who are ultimately left totally alone."
JUDITH MCCOMBS, THE HABIT OF *FIRE: POEMS SELECTED & NEW*

"With all the dread-filled propulsion of certain dreams, Mike Maggio's *The Appointment* runs on urgency. No time to get a grip on what just happened or what adds up: Professor Withers has been wounded somehow, and yet he still strives for agency and meaning, as though the powers of officialdom were not driving him relentlessly towards the appointed end."
MADELEINE MYSKO, *BRINGING VINCENT HOME* AND *STONE HARBOR BOUND*

"Mike Maggio has one of the weirdest minds I've ever come across, and like all weird minds it is fascinating, colourful, dramatic, and hilarious. Read, laugh, ponder."
SOPHY BURNHAM, AUTHOR OF *LOVE, ALBA*

ABOUT THE AUTHOR

Mike Maggio has published fiction, poetry, travel and reviews in, *The Montserrat Review, Pleiades, Apalachee Quarterly, The Northern Virginia Review, The L.A. Weekly, The Washington CityPaper, Beltway Quarterly, Pig Iron, DC Poets Against the War, Washington Independent Review of Books* and many others. He is an assistant professor at Northern Virginia Community College, an associate editor at *Potomac Review*, a graduate of George Mason University's MFA program in Creative Writing and the Northern Regional Vice-President of the Poetry Society of Virginia.

Visit his website: *mikemaggio.net*

Print Edition
ISBN: 978-1-925417-34-0
Published by Vine Leaves Press 2017
Melbourne, Victoria, Australia

This is a work of fiction. Any similarity between the characters and situations within its pages and places or persons, living or dead, is unintentional and coincidental.

Cover design by Jessica Bell
Interior design by Amie McCracken

National Library of Australia Cataloguing-in-Publication entry (pbk)
Creator: Maggio, Mike, author.
Title: The appointment / Mike Maggio.
ISBN: 9781925417340 (paperback)
Subjects: Alienation (Social psychology)--Fiction.
Bureaucracy--Fiction.

THE APPOINTMENT

MIKE MAGGIO

Vine Leaves Press
Melbourne, Vic, Australia

ALSO BY MIKE MAGGIO

Fiction:
Sifting Through the Madness
The Keepers
The Wizard and the White House

Poetry:
Your Secret Is Safe With Me
Oranges From Palestine
deMockcracy
Garden of Rain

CHAPTER 1

Professor Jeremy Withers eased himself up on his elbow and touched the back of his neck with a trembling hand. Returning it to his hazy field of vision, his head heavy and aching, he stared at his blood-soaked fingers and wondered what had happened to bring him to this numb, bewildered state.

He recalled waiting for the train. That's all. A memory that emerged from the shadows, disappeared into the black abyss, became lost in a swash of cumbersome thoughts that slowly materialized into his consciousness: A.M., rush hour, 7:05.

He was on his way to the college to grade his final exams. That much he remembered.

There was calm.

Then shouting.

Chaos.

The kind that can only happen on a packed subway platform, when danger suddenly erupts and there is nowhere to turn. The silent panic.

The feeble attempts to ignore—*punks? skinheads? street gangs?*—as they emerged like ghosts, heads shaved, arms tattooed, brandishing knives and chains and shoving people out of their way.

Fearful, he buried himself in his newspaper.

Anonymity is the best defence.

He had seen it in a magazine, or perhaps a friend had said it.

He tried to read, but his eyes froze: *Monday, December 4, 1995.* That's all that would register.

Monday, December 4, 1995, 7:05.

Then they were on him.

Merciless.

They knocked him around, smashed his head again and again against the steel pillar he had been leaning on.

Why had they chosen him?

He remembered his book bag spilling onto the subway platform. He remembered begging them to let him live. He remembered reaching feebly for his hat as it flew off his head and landed on the tracks, just before his vision went blank, just as a train came screeching into the station.

My hat, please, my hat!

Professor Withers' elbow ached from the hardness of the concrete platform. He slid down onto his back and tried to get the words out of his mind—*my hat*—but they echoed back at him as if he were in a dark tunnel and he had just shouted them. *My hat. My hat.* He wished the terrible sounds would stop. He wished he could trap them, put them in an airtight container and seal it so they would cease haunting him.

He opened his eyes again and looked up. Blurred faces stared down at him from the dingy station—strangers suddenly concerned, their faces distorted and ghostly, their voices an incoherent mumble.

"My hat!"

But they didn't seem to hear him, or perhaps they didn't care. And why should they? They had watched him get beaten up and had not made any attempt to help. What would it matter now that he had lost the one possession that meant more to him than anything else! What difference could it possibly make to them that he had sworn, as his mother was breathing her last, that he would wear the hat she had given him on his fifty-fourth birthday until his very own death.

"My hat!" he shouted again.

But they just kept talking as if he didn't exist, in a language that made no sense, in strange sounds that blended in with the roar of a train fading into the distance.

Then, miraculously, Professor Withers felt better. Not that he was religious. Far from it. But the transformation that occurred was so rapid and so dramatic, he immediately understood what it was that made people believe in God. The pain in his head ceased, and his vision abruptly cleared up.

At first he was so shocked, he lay there waiting for something else to happen. Then he sat up, his head light as a balloon, so light he thought he might float away.

Perhaps this was what happened when you died, he thought. Perhaps the sudden clarity, the inexplicable feeling that everything you had done in life was suddenly available for review— perhaps all of this was a sign that he was about to enter another life—another dimension.

Professor Withers got up on his feet. He took a close look at the crowd that had gathered around him, their faces an eerie chiaroscuro under the bald subway lighting. Tears came to his eyes. He wanted to thank them for their concern. He wanted to let them know that everything was all right and they could now get on with their lives. But just then his train pulled into the station—a beautiful, new, shining train—and he took his leave and boarded.

CHAPTER 2

When Professor Withers arrived at his subway stop, he stood on the platform and watched the train disappear down the dark tunnel. Then he climbed up the worn stairs of the gloomy station. The light feeling that had overcome him when he first boarded the subway car was gone, snatched away as fast as the train pulled away. Now, each movement was heavy and cumbersome, and he stopped to catch his breath and rest his limbs.

Out on the street, the fresh December air embraced him. He took a deep breath, closed his eyes, filled his lungs with the soothing coolness, then slumped against the graffitied wall and listened to his heart throb like an old pump ready to wheeze to a halt. His legs tingled, his hands, stiff and heavy, could barely sense the worn, age-tainted banister he now grasped for support. Numb and bewildered, like he had been given some strange drug, he struggled to get his eyes to focus.

A cold wind grazed his bare head. Out of habit, he reached for his hat. Then he remembered—realized, like someone gradually emerging from a cloud of anaesthesia——what had happened. He had been attacked. Had nearly died. He could barely comprehend how he had survived.

"I'm alive!" he said aloud, and his voice echoed through the vacant plaza.

Professor Withers gazed up at the gloomy sky and pressed on towards the college. A quiet buzzing filled his head, an odd cloud veiled his vision. He walked, unsure as he stepped down on one foot whether he would have the strength to lift the other. Buildings loomed before him, huge and lopsided, swelling and shrinking with each step. The narrow sidewalk wound endlessly like a mysterious maze. He leaned on street poles, grabbed hold of benches, and grappled at bushes and trees as he slowly made his way towards the campus.

When he reached the main gate, he stopped to rest his racing heart. Frightened, he wondered if he should call a doctor, and he pushed on, delirious yet determined to reach his office, making his way across the deserted campus until he reached the building where his department was located.

He struggled up the darkened stairway, wandered like a lost child through empty hallways, then approached the door to his office and heaved a deep sigh of relief.

Here, at last, he thought, in his cluttered little room, he would rest a bit. Then he would determine how to proceed.

He unlocked the door and opened it and turned on the light. Then, as if his soul had been snatched away, he let out a cry that echoed off the hard surface of the bare walls and stared in disbelief. Everything was gone: his books, the clutter that always filled his desk, the bookshelves he had fought so hard for when he'd first starting teaching, the manuscript he had been working on for the past thirty years. In their stead stood an empty desk, pushed over to the side of the room, and an old, wooden chair, worn from years of use, sitting in the corner.

Professor Withers closed the door behind him. Stunned, he gazed at the vacant room, trying to comprehend the emptiness that stared back at him, then forced himself over to the desk and eased himself down onto the cold, hard chair.

Had he entered the wrong office? Or had he just gone mad? He removed his scarf and gloves, unbuttoned his coat, closed his eyes as tight as he could. Surely, this must be a dream. Surely, he would soon wake up and reflect, over a cup of strong black coffee, on the meaning of this terrible nightmare.

But before he could contemplate any further, there came a loud knocking on his office door.

"Yes," he said.

His voice was thin and raspy, as if it had no substance, as if, like everything else, it had been snatched away. He opened his eyes, watched, helplessly—a man whose actions no longer seemed to have any consequence, whose existence had been suddenly challenged—as the door swung open on its creaky hinges, revealing two men hovering in the dimly lit hallway. Dressed in black suits and wearing dark glasses, eclipsed by the bright light that flooded his office, they seemed alike, though one stood tall and upright and had a face that appeared to be chiselled from stone.

"Jeremy Randolph Withers?"

"Yes," he said, his voice as insubstantial as the two figures that seemed to float mirage-like in the doorway.

"We've come to investigate the disturbance."

Bewildered, Professor Withers stared as the second individual, a short, squat fellow with a distant countenance, asked if they could come in. Without waiting for an answer, they stepped inside and closed the door behind them.

"You have a right to remain silent," the short man began.

"Why would I want to remain silent? I need to report a crime."

"That's not for us to say. We have our orders. We just do as we're told. May we have your identification, please?"

"I don't have any ID," Professor Withers said, reaching into his empty pocket.

"No ID," the man repeated. "Mark that down, Agent Smith."

"I've been robbed," Professor Withers said. "Everything was taken from me. My wallet. My credits cards."

"No credit cards," the short man said as Agent Smith scribbled in his little black notebook.

"May I ask what this is about?"

"We'll do the questioning," Agent Smith said.

"Excuse me," Professor Withers said, suddenly indignant. "I've been victimized. Don't I have any rights?"

"Professor Withers," Agent Smith said with impatience. "Your rights will be duly given to you. Now please cooperate."

Professor Withers eyed the two men. He had not yet called the police, he realized. Why had these two men shown up? he wondered. Just like that. And how, he thought, had they found him in the first place?

"May I see your badges, please?" he asked at last.

The two men withdrew black leather folders from their coat pockets and held up their ID's for Professor Withers to see.

"'Agent John Smith'," he read out loud, "'Bureau of Rectification—Special Investigations. Agent Simon LeFabvre, Bureau of Rectification—Special Investigations.' This is a joke, right? My students set you up to this."

"This is no joke, Professor Withers. You will need to come with us so everything can be settled."

Professor Withers grinned at the two strangers, but their unflinching stares caught him off guard.

"OK. But before I answer any more questions, I'll need to call a lawyer."

"Professor Withers," Agent LeFabvre said. "There's no need for representation."

"You treat me like a common criminal and you say there's no need for representation?"

"Things are not so simple, Professor Withers. This is a very serious matter."

"Yes, it is. I was attacked on the subway this morning. I was beaten and left for dead. And now you come and treat me as if *I've* committed a crime."

"We understand your quandary," Agent Smith said. "It's quite common at this stage."

"Quandary? Stage?"

Professor Withers stared at the two men.

"Professor Withers. We have come to help you," Agent LeFabvre said. "We have come to rectify your situation and we will. But you have to cooperate."

"Leave my office at once," Professor Withers shouted. "Leave my office or I will call security."

The two agents looked at one another.

"It will do no good," Agent Smith said.

"Leave at once or I will call security," Professor Withers said.

"Very well," Agent LeFabvre said. "We understand. These situations can be very trying. We will leave for now. But you cannot escape us. Your situation must be rectified. Sooner or later you will have to come to terms." Agent LeFabvre swept the office with an open hand. "As you can see, there is nothing left here for you."

"Please leave me," Professor Withers said. "Just leave me."

"Very well. But we will meet again. Good day, Professor Jeremy Randolph Withers."

And with that, the two men disappeared down the long, narrow hallway.

CHAPTER 3

Professor Withers closed his office door and leaned against it for support as Agent LeFabvre's words reverberated through his head. Slowly, he surveyed the empty room. Everything had been removed: his books, his files, the manuscript he had been working on for the last ten years. His life's work had been taken. Disappeared. Innocent victims of an absurd event he could not comprehend. Agent LeFabvre, he concluded, as he stared in disbelief at the sudden void he was confronted with, was right about one thing: there *was* nothing left for him.

His body began to tremble again. He walked over to the empty chair and sat down, held his hands out and watched them quiver. His body was weak, his mind paralyzed. He could not explain what had happened, did not know who could possibly be behind this inexplicable event. He closed his eyes and took a deep breath, tried to make sense of everything that had occurred since the morning. Unable to calm himself, he steadied his hands by placing them under his legs, putting the full pressure of his body on them and rocking himself back and forth as tears rolled down his leathery cheeks. He concentrated on the silence that filled the room, a void that seemed to swallow him as if nothing else existed but this quiet emptiness.

Then, his thoughts came into focus, and he stopped rocking. Nothing changes without action. It was a basic philosophical tenet. A wheel does not turn unless it is acted upon. It could be a person, an animal, even the wind, but something has to cause the wheel to spin. That was the example he had always given his students. Action produces action. Stasis is a result of inaction. He had come to his office and found it empty. Someone had taken action to cause this. His chairman, perhaps. The Dean. Maybe, even, his students, playing a prank. Now, he thought, he would have to find out.

Professor Withers reached for his coat and scarf. He would go straight to the Dean, he thought, as he readied himself for the cold. He would demand an explanation.

Professor Withers left his office and made his way across campus as fast as his feeble legs would allow. A harsh wind howled between the buildings and penetrated his bones. Though it was only mid-December, it felt like the dead of winter. A light, chilling rain was falling, and the last of the leaves swirled about him like little brown whirlwinds.

Cautiously, he approached the Dean's building. Inside, he removed his gloves, ran his hand through his thick hair and smoothed his grizzled beard so he would look presentable.

The hallways were dark and deserted, and Professor Withers' footsteps echoed as he wound his way towards the Dean's office. When he arrived, he tapped his feeble fingers on the huge, wooden door, then tried the doorknob and found that it would not budge.

Professor Withers peered through the bevelled glass panel that looked into the Dean's suite and spotted Miss Watkins, the Dean's secretary, huddled over her desk. He knocked again, this time with more force, and waited in vain for her to respond, until he found himself pounding so heavily and yelling so loudly that it sounded as if the building was under construction.

At last, Miss Watkins stood up and made her way towards the door. She opened it, looked up and down the hallway with a blank look on her face, and sighed. Shrugging her shoulders, she closed the door and returned to her desk.

"Miss Watkins," Professor Withers shouted, banging his fist on the door again. "Are you blind as well as deaf? Miss Watkins!"

As he pounded against the door, his anger subsided and he detected the faint sound of footsteps coming down the hallway. Turning, he saw the Dean heading towards him and he smiled, but the Dean proceeded right past him, opening the door and closing it behind him as he entered his office.

Professor Withers stood for a moment with a puzzled look on his face, then tried the doorknob once again but it still refused to budge.

Action produces action. He repeated the phrase as if to convince himself. Then, unable to control himself, he let out a shriek that echoed throughout the hollow hallway.

CHAPTER 4

Moments passed as Professor Withers stood in the darkened doorway and tried to get a grip on himself. His nerves were shattered, and he could no longer make sense of the things that were taking place around him: strange events that made him now question his very existence. Had the Dean simply ignored him? Hadn't Miss Watkins heard him banging on the door? And who were those two individuals who had visited him in his office? Were they real or figments of his imagination, ghosts conjured up by an insidious attack of stress that seemed to be getting the better of him?

And then he recalled the events that had taken place just the day before, things he had brushed off as just misunderstanding or a prank played by a disgruntled student. He had been sitting in his office, trying to grade his exams, when he received a phone call from the Dean, summoning him immediately for a meeting. He remembered putting on his coat, fumbling for his hat and gloves, rushing through the wind and cold and arriving, out of breath, at the Dean's office.

At first, Miss Watkins had just ignored him as he burst into the room, but then she looked up at him in that way she had that told him he was not welcome—scrutinized him through squinted eyes as she tapped her tapered nails impatiently against the blank manila folder that lay closed before her on her desk. She sat bent over with her usual dour expression, her back slightly curved and her head protruding sinisterly, and Professor Withers decided, right then and there, as he waited in silence for her to acknowledge his presence, that she was not at all unlike a snake. It was not so much her small, round face and her flat featureless nose, but the way she glared silently whenever you entered the office, like a cobra mesmerizing its prey, ready to pounce at the least provocation.

"May I help you?" she asked at last, in her nasal voice.

"I have an appointment with the Dean," Professor Withers said hesitating, not wanting to provoke her, not wanting her to snap as she always did.

"I beg your pardon!" she answered, peering at him from beneath the rim of her pointed glasses as if she needed to get a different view of him, her mouth hung wide like she had just seen a ghost.

"Did I hear you correctly?" she asked. "That the Dean wants to see you?"

"Yes, Miss Watkins."

"Well, I can assure you, *Professor*, that you are

mistaken. I keep all the Dean's appointments, and I most certainly do not have one for you."

"Miss Watkins. The Dean himself just called me —"

"Professor Withers," Miss Watkins said—hissed, really, he thought now, as he stood outside in the hallway and recalled what had happened. "Don't you understand? If the Dean wished to see you, I would have been informed. Now, since I have no knowledge of this so-called meeting, I think it's safe to assume that one hasn't been scheduled. Good day, Professor Withers!"

And with that, she resumed her work, pored mindlessly over the papers scattered across her desk as if he didn't exist, as if he had never even entered the room.

Professor Withers remembered wiping away the beads of sweat that appeared on his brow. He remembered his heart beating, his hands shaking. And now, as he stood trembling, once again, outside the Dean's office, staring at Miss Watkins through the murky glass, he couldn't help but think that it was, perhaps, the beginning of something more serious: a nervous breakdown, maybe, though he had never understood what that term actually meant.

"Miss Watkins," he said, "the Dean just called me a few minutes ago. I rushed across campus as quickly as I could. If you could just check with him. If it's no trouble, that is."

"No," she said, her nostrils inflating. "No trouble at all. I have nothing better to do. Have a seat, Professor."

Professor Withers sat in the stiff wooden chair in the corner of the room as Miss Watkins stomped into the Dean's office, barely able to balance herself on her spiked high heels. He remembered a sudden bout of anxiety. He remembered wondering, as he waited, what the Dean could possibly want. He remembered tapping his foot on the floor, recalling the rumours that circulated around campus: how the Dean would summon unwitting staff members into his office; how he would confront them for alleged ineptitudes; how he would frighten the weaker of them into submission. After all, he was a hunter, and, as the story went, he approached his subordinates the same way he did the animals he pursued, stalking them until he was ready to open fire. As Professor Withers waited for Miss Watkins to return, he wondered whether he was the next victim on the list, though he could not imagine what he might have done to earn the Dean's ire.

The door to the Dean's office opened and Miss Watkins reappeared, the look on her meagre face more dour than before.

"You may go in, Professor. The Dean will see you."

"Thank you," Professor Withers said. "Sorry to trouble you."

"No trouble at all."

Professor Withers composed himself, then knocked on the Dean's door and stepped into the large, dimly-lit chamber. It took several seconds for his eyes to adjust but, when they did, he was satisfied to see that at least one of the rumours he had heard about the Dean was true, for there, suspended in one corner of the room, was the head of a vicious lion poised to pounce, while in the other, a large rhino trophy glared at him, as if ready for the attack. At last, he recognized the figure of the Dean, seated behind a large, imposing desk, the smoke from his thick cigar curling up and disappearing into nowhere.

"Professor Withers," the Dean said, breaking the silence and standing up to shake hands. "How nice to see you," he said, with a curious look on his face. "Please. Have a seat."

"Thank you," Professor Withers said, shrinking into the huge chair that faced the Dean's desk.

"It isn't often department members come to visit me," the Dean said, adjusting the glasses on his pointed face. "One would think I had a contagious disease or some such rot. So, how's the teaching going?"

"Just fine, sir."

"Anything we can do to help?"

"No. Nothing at all."

"Glad to hear it."

Professor Withers waited in silence for the Dean to continue. He rubbed his sweaty hands on his knee caps as the Dean thumped his fingers on his desk and examined him, as if he were trying to process the individual sitting before him into a formula that could sum him up into one complete result.

"Good," the Dean said, clearing his throat. "Well, then, what's on your mind, old boy?"

"Sir?"

"Miss Watkins said you needed to see me."

Professor Withers stared at the Dean. His heart began to race, his hands trembled, and he felt as if the room were closing in on him.

"Are you all right, Withers?"

Professor Withers gripped the arms of his chair for support and tried to focus on the painting hung behind the Dean's desk—a curious scene of a hunter stalking some animal that was off-canvas—but his vision kept going blurry on him.

"Shall I call a doctor?"

"No," Professor Withers said. "I'll be all right."

"It's the stress, Withers. The end of the semester. Exams to mark. Students worried about their grades. Pressure from all sides. Almost like hunting, you know. You have to remain alert or the animal will get you first. Frankly, Withers, you look awful. Like you've been through the mill. You ought to take a rest over the holidays. Go somewhere. You're not getting any younger, you know?"

The Dean chuckled as if what he had just said were strikingly funny.

"Yes, perhaps you're right," Professor Withers responded.

"Of course I'm right. Well, thanks for the visit. Sorry

to rush you, but I do have an appointment. Busy schedule, you know. Hope you feel better, Withers."

"Thank you, sir."

Professor Withers stood and made his way to the door, then turned once again towards the Dean.

"Sir?"

"Yes, Withers," the Dean answered, looking up from his desk.

"I was just wondering," he began. "I was wondering if—."

Professor Withers could not complete the sentence. It was absurd, he thought, asking the Dean to confirm whether he had called him on the phone.

"Well, Withers, what is it? I haven't got all day, you know."

"I was just wondering," he began again, not quite sure what to say, now that he had begun. "Well," he said at last, "I was wondering if I could wish you a Merry Christmas."

"Why, of course you may. And a very Happy New Year to you. Now you go home and get some rest and you'll feel a lot better. And don't let those students get to you like this."

"Yes, sir."

Professor Withers recalled leaving the Dean's office feeling foolish and wondering which of his students could be behind this embarrassing incident. Perhaps Jason, he had thought at the time. After all, he had failed the midterm. Or maybe Matt who had told him in front of everyone how worthless he thought philosophy was.

"I hope you're satisfied, Professor," Miss Watkins said, noticing the troubled expression on his face as he walked past her desk. "Because that's the last time you'll get to see the Dean without an appointment," she called after him as he walked towards the door. "Do you understand?"

"Yes," he said, stepping into the hallway. "I do appreciate your help. Merry Christmas, Miss Watkins."

"Merry Christmas, indeed!"

So now, as he stood in the hallway, trying to make sense of these strange events—trying to make sense of all the bizarre events that were now suddenly taking place, one after the other— he began to wonder if they had actually occurred, if, perhaps, he had been imagining it all or if he were inside a dream from which he found it impossible to escape.

CHAPTER 5

Late that afternoon, Professor Withers headed for home, his students' final exams untouched, his bare head numb from the cold that grabbed and shook him as he lumbered like a wounded animal down the deserted street, his mind weary from trying to piece together the events that had happened to him over the past couple of days.

Perhaps the Dean had been right, he thought, wincing and stiffening against the blustery wind that blew with unleashed fury. He did need a vacation. It had been years since he had gotten away and taken his mind off his work, and then it had always been with his mother to the same summer spa where they would sit on the beach, she to revive her failing health under the sun's therapeutic rays and he to wade through the books he had not gotten to all year. A vacation would do him good. A true vacation, by himself, where he did only what he wanted to do. Perhaps he would go to Florida. Or just sit around the house, catching up on old magazines or watching TV.

Still, Professor Withers remained unconvinced that he was merely suffering from fatigue, and he approached the subway station, like a frightened child who had become lost, who, trying to restrain his tears, wondered if he would ever find his way back home.

After waiting on the deserted platform for what seemed an eternity, Professor Withers boarded his train and took a seat on the cold, hard bench. He wanted to close his eyes and go to sleep. He wanted to forget everything that had happened to him that day, wake up refreshed and invigorated, magically transported back to his apartment, his hat still hanging in the corner, his morning paper waiting to be read. He would get up, go to his office and find it as cluttered and messy as he had left it the last time he had turned off the lights and headed for home. But instead, his mind kept skipping back and forth like a scratched LP, analyzing over and over each detail of the nightmare that had suddenly become his life.

Frustrated, Professor Withers tried to distract himself by concentrating on the clack and echo of the train roaring through the darkness, on the flickering subway lights which caught his attention and began to soothe him.

Then, for the first time since he had boarded the train, Professor Withers looked around and realized he was alone. It was four in the afternoon, and the train was empty. Surprised, he began to wonder where the crowds could be, wondered how, on a weekday after-noon, he could find himself riding by himself on the subway through the middle of town.

"Take a vacation, Withers. You're not getting any younger."

The voice startled him.

"But—"

Professor Withers looked around in a panic, but the subway car was as empty as his office had been.

"But, but. There are no buts, Withers. When I say take a vacation, you do so."

"But I need answers," he cried out.

His hands were trembling and a sudden chill rushed through his body. He stood up, took hold of a strap hanger, and peered directly down the length of the subway car.

"I need answers!"

"It's all immaterial, Withers. Immaterial. Now get a move on, you hear, before I get my gun and put you out of your misery."

Professor Withers heard a loud bang as the empty subway car clattered through the dark tunnel. He wanted to run. He wanted to escape from this horrible nightmare that had become his life, but, trapped in this speeding subway car, there was no way out, so he turned and stared out the window, his face frozen in fear. A crowded express train came cruising down the centre track. He watched as it meshed with his, then struggled to pull away, the rhythmic flicker of window against window mesmerizing him as the express train picked up speed. At last it broke free and gradually diminished into the darkness, as Professor Withers noticed two figures waving at him from the back window of the last car.

"11 o'clock tomorrow" they yelled above the roar. "Be there, or else."

CHAPTER 6

When he reached his station, Professor Withers rushed up the stairs and hurried towards his apartment. He wanted to lock himself in his room, close the curtains, turn out the lights and bury himself in his bed. But even as he walked the same streets he had taken for most of his life, even as he tried to take comfort from the shops he had patronized for so long, from the boulevard which had remained mostly unchanged throughout the long stretch of time he had lived in the neighbourhood, he felt as if something was suddenly different and, though he could not quite define it, he detected a strange aura in the air. The streets were quiet, and even though it had stopped raining, the sidewalks, normally bustling with pedestrians at this time of the afternoon, were mysteriously devoid of life. Even the children, whom he encountered almost daily without fail, strolling with their mothers or running among the patches of green that chequered the sidewalks, were absent. An eerie silence enveloped the quarter like an ominous cocoon, an odd emptiness chilled him even more than the cold wind that was blowing, as if the entire city had taken flight and he had been left alone.

Professor Withers approached the gate to his building and realized, as he shoved his hand into his empty pocket, that he no longer had his key, so he buzzed Mr. Beasley, the apartment manager, and waited, shifting from one foot to the other in an effort to keep warm. A minute later, he pushed the button again and drummed his finger nervously on the call box.

He was about to leave to find a warm place—where, he was not sure, for the loose change in his pocket would not buy him even a cup of coffee—when his neighbour's daughter came skipping out of the building.

"Laura," he called out to her, waving his hand in the air.

The little girl stopped and looked around, then went running off through the courtyard and out of sight.

"Laura!" he yelled again.

Dismayed though he was, he consoled himself with the realization that the girl's mother would at least be home, so he rang her apartment and waited for her to answer.

As he was about to give up, Mrs. Brown, his mother's long-time friend, appeared at the end of the block. Weighed down by packages and old age, she was cobbling her way up the street—a relic from another time, he thought, as he watched her inch her way towards him, a skeleton of a woman who seemed barely alive as she inched her way up the deserted boulevard, keeping her callused eyes on him as she approached the dilapidated building.

Professor Withers forced a smile through his shivering lips and held out his hand to offer assistance.

"Go away!" she cried, clutching her purse against her chest. "Leave me alone!"

"Mrs. Brown, it's me," Professor Withers assured her. "Jeremy."

"Jeremy? Jeremy who?"

She extended her wrinkled face forward like a buzzard and eyed him menacingly, her pale countenance a ghostly mask, her gaping mouth revealing a maw of sparse, crooked teeth.

"Jeremy," he repeated. "Jeremy Withers."

"Jeremy Withers? You ain't Jeremy Withers. Jeremy Withers is dead!"

Professor Withers felt weak as Mrs. Brown began to laugh, her hollow voice reverberating through the empty courtyard. Then she stopped, pointed a bony finger at him and said in a hoarse whisper:

"Jeremy Withers died two weeks ago. Saw it with my own eyes. Died just before the medics came. Just before the train car struck me."

Mrs. Brown cackled again, as Professor Withers lost his balance and fell against the apartment gate. He lifted his hands in the air, examined them, then turned again to his spectre of a neighbour.

"Mrs. Brown. I'm alive. Can't you see?"

"Did you hear what I said?" she insisted, shoving the gate open with her shoulder. "Jeremy Withers is gone. Now you go away and leave us poor dead folk to rest."

Mrs. Brown grabbed her packages and skittered across the courtyard, disappearing into the black portal of the run-down building.

Professor Withers was able to get through the gate before it closed, and he headed straight for the lobby, his heart pounding, his hands sweating from fear, his footsteps echoing against the tiled surface of the dimly-lit foyer.

When the elevator arrived, Professor Withers pushed the call button and waited to reach his floor. As it slowly creaked its way up, Mrs. Brown's words reverberated through his mind, and he examined his hands again. Perhaps she hadn't recognized him, he thought. Perhaps old age was finally getting to her. Dementia was setting in, and she could no longer remember things. After all, he reasoned, she was nearly ninety.

When the elevator came to a stop, he stepped into the diffused light of the hallway. As he walked towards his apartment, a cold, empty feeling overcame him. It was as if a hundred eyes were resting heavily on him, watching him, examining him, as if, instead of moving of his own free will, he were being carried through the long dark corridor. Making his way forward, he detected faint sounds, voices whispering incomprehensibly and, through it all, the hushed echo of someone wailing. Yet, as he looked around, he could see that the corridor was vacant, and the silence became so still again that the fact that he had neighbours was not at all evident.

As Professor Withers turned the doorknob of his apartment door, a dull creaking echoed through the dreary hallway and he noticed, from the corner of his eye, Mrs. Jacobs, the old recluse who lived in the next unit, peeking through her doorway. As their eyes met, she quickly slammed the door shut and locked it, the sound of her door chain rattling through the empty hallway.

"Mrs. Jacobs," he called, his voice echoing through the emptiness.

Professor Withers rushed into his apartment and went straight to the bathroom where he examined himself in the mirror. His hair, he could now see, was totally dishevelled from the wind, and his beard was wild and unkempt. No wonder Mrs. Brown had not recognized him! he thought, as he dragged a comb across his head. No wonder Mrs. Jacobs had slammed the door in his face! But he soon realized that the problem went beyond his scruffy appearance, for his face seemed lifeless and drawn and his skin had a sallow tone to it. Moving closer to the mirror, he could see that his eyes had gone puffy and sagged heavily, and the wrinkles on his face had become dry and cracked. His countenance, it appeared, had changed so much that his reflection seemed to bear no resemblance to his former self.

Professor Withers pressed his hands against his face to make sure there was still substance. He touched the mirror, the faucet, the sink, trying to convince himself that he was, indeed, alive.

Just then, the telephone rang, and Professor Withers hurried into the living room.

"Yes," he said, pressing the receiver to his ear.

"11 A.M. sharp," the voice on the other end said. "Be there."

Professor Withers gasped as the line went dead. With a cry of alarm, he hung up the phone and sank into his worn-out armchair.

CHAPTER 7

The next day, after a night of turbulent dreams, Professor Withers put on his clothes and headed for the college. It was snowing when he left his apartment and, by the time he emerged from the subway, a ghostly pallor had engulfed the city. Trudging through the blinding snow, he checked his watch as he approached the campus, fearful he would miss his appointed time. At exactly eleven o'clock, as the second hand touched twelve, he arrived at his office and waited for the two mysterious inspectors to appear.

At twenty past the hour, his eyes sunken and his body weary from lack of sleep, Professor Withers began to relax. Surely, he thought, he was in the clear. If they hadn't shown up by now, it only proved that this whole unpleasant affair was nothing more than a sick joke. So he tried to push it out of his mind and proceed with more pressing matters. Opening his book bag, he began to retrieve his unmarked exams when he noticed a flimsy note, stuck to the side of his desk, beckoning him with a flutter:

**The Dean wants to see you. For real this time!
11:30 on the dot. DO NOT keep him waiting.**

Professor Withers wondered whether this was yet another hoax, and he considered phoning Miss Watkins but decided that the tone of the message was so consistent with her curt, sardonic style that it had to be authentic. So he threw on his coat and gloves and rushed across the snow-covered campus, nearly slipping on the icy sidewalk and trying his utmost to remain calm.

When he reached the Dean's office, the door was wide open, and Miss Watkins sat waiting in her chair with an especially menacing look draped across her pitiful, gloomy face, like a vulture ready to pounce on its prey. Shifting back and forth, she flipped through papers scattered across her desk, as Professor Withers stared, her image coming into focus, then fading into a blur, as if he were looking at her through a sliver of dense glass.

"Well, Professor," she said, looking up. "I see you got my message. And good thing you got here on time. The Dean's a busy man, you know."

She set her brooding eyes on him and puffed her mouth until Professor Withers thought it might explode.

"Well," she squawked at last, flapping her arms. "What are you waiting for? Time is precious. Go on in. Go on in."

Miss Watkins hunched her shoulders and hopped down from her chair as the door to the Dean's office swung open. Apprehensive, Professor Withers stepped into the dark, sunless room.

"Come on in then. Don't dawdle. Have a seat."

Professor Withers groped through the terrible darkness until he found the chair he had occupied during his last visit.

"Sorry to bother you, old boy, but I do have a serious matter to discuss with you."

The Dean leaned over his enormous desk, a huge man diminished by perspective, his face meagre, his arms long and sinuous. Behind him on the wall hung the painting Professor Withers had taken note of during his previous visit, the animal lying in a pool of blood which glistened as if it were still fresh. He thought he detected something moving across the canvas, but a massive stack of papers fell onto the desk with a loud thump that shot through the darkness and obscured the image from his vision.

"I've been going over your file, Withers. Routine, you know. I review them every few minutes, as time allows. I see that, with one or two exceptions, you've gotten miserable evaluations from your students."

"Sir?"

"I'll do the talking, Withers," the Dean shouted.

He stretched his head over the mound of paper until Professor Withers thought it would snap off.

"Your publications since your tenure have been sparse. Almost nil. Though you have placed a number of them in several rather obscure journals."

The Dean raised his voice and buckled his brow.

"Obscurity, Withers! Obscurity. But that's not my concern. My concern is your blatant disrespect for policy."

"Policy?"

"Policy. It's standard policy, as you know Withers, that professors may arrive to class as late as twenty minutes into the session. After that, students are free to leave. But surely you are aware of that."

"Yes—."

"But are you also aware that this professor's privilege—if I may call it that—of showing up willy-nilly—is to be used sparingly?"

"Sir?"

"It has come to my attention, Withers, that you did not show up for class for the last two weeks of the semester. In fact, according to your file, you did not even show up to administer the final exam."

The Dean thrust his head forward, extending his neck until it seemed to dangle in the air like a taut jack-in-the-box.

"That's not true," Professor Withers said.

"Not true? Not true!"

"I have not been absent for class at all this semester and I was most certainly there for the final exam."

"Then where are your grades, Withers?" the Dean asked, his head springing back onto his shoulders.

"I haven't had a chance to grade them yet. I've—."

"You haven't graded them?"

"I've been trying to get to them, but—"

"Withers. The grades were due this morning at eleven o'clock."

"Today?"

"Yes. It clearly states on the calendar that grades are due on the twentieth. And today is the twentieth."

"The twentieth? But—."

"Look Withers. I don't have time to argue. Now it's true that I can't fire you. You *are* fully tenured. But I can make life damn miserable for you if you don't cooperate. Have I made myself clear?"

Professor Withers stared at the Dean in response.

"Damn miserable, Withers," the Dean repeated several times more until the words began to echo through the darkness.

"Thank you, Withers," the Dean said at last. "Do have a good day."

And with that, he stood, turned, and walked towards the wall, disappearing into the lifeless canvas.

Professor Withers left the Dean's office feeling numb. In all his years of teaching, he had never been spoken to in such a manner, and to be told that today was the twentieth when he was sure that it was only the fifth—.

"Good meeting, Professor?" Miss Watkins chirped as he walked by her desk.

"Miss Watkins," he said, turning towards her. "Can you tell me what day it is?"

"Why of course Professor. It's Wednesday, December twentieth."

"Are you sure?"

"Quite. Not finished with your Christmas shopping? Not to worry. You still have the weekend."

"Yes," he said. "Of course. Thank you, Miss Watkins."

"Not at all," she said as he walked off. "Better get those exams graded, Professor," she called after him. "Merry Christmas."

CHAPTER 8

What disturbed Professor Withers the most was not so much how unprofessionally he had been treated, but rather how the Dean and Miss Watkins had conspired together in fabricating such a ridiculous story. The Dean must have taken an immediate disliking to him the day before and, since there was nothing out of form in his file, had secured Miss Watkins' assistance in helping to discredit him.

Yet, as if he were still not convinced how absurd this incredible fabrication seemed, Professor Withers found himself repeating, over and over, in a shrill voice which echoed across the deserted campus as he rushed back to his office, that there was no way he could have missed two weeks of class.

Breathless, Professor Withers arrived at last at his empty room, his heart racing, his body trembling from fear and cold. As he removed his coat and gloves, another message, stuck to the side of his desk, caught his attention:

You missed your appointed time. You are now required to report at three o'clock. Failure to do so will not weigh in your favour. Regards, Agent Simon LeFabvre, Bureau of Rectification— Special Investigations.

Professor Withers wanted to cry out but could not muster up the strength. As he struggled to get a grip on his seemingly failing sanity, he noticed the date of the message: 12-20-95 11:33:05.

"How can that be?"

Professor Withers needed answers. He needed them now or he would go mad. That's how it starts, he thought: slowly, inconspicuously. Then it grows— insidiously, barely detectable by the individual —and before you know it, you're branded, condemned, institutionalized, and you never find out what really happened. Or, even, who you truly are.

"How can today be December twentieth?"

Frantic, Professor Withers reached for the telephone book on his desk and searched for Agent LeFabvre's number. He was the key, he concluded, to all that was happening, though he could not explain why. He just knew it, like a mother knows her infant child, like an animal, in its deepest hunger, knows exactly where to find food. LeFabvre would have the answers, would be able to clarify Mrs. Brown's irrational reaction to him, would be able to explain the Dean's sudden and bizarre outburst, would be able to tell him how today, the twentieth of December, in the year nineteen hundred and ninety five, was not December fifth as he had believed, and how he, a conscientious educator who, throughout his many years of teaching, had been absent for, perhaps, only three days of class, could wake up and suddenly find out that he had missed two entire weeks of the semester.

Professor Withers' search was fruitless. He found listings for the Bureau of Alcohol, Tobacco and Fire-arms, the Bureau of Engraving, the Bureau of Indian Affairs and the Bureau of the Budget. Perhaps it was his impatience that caused his finger to jump across the page, or perhaps it was the outdated telephone book, but as hard as he looked, as hard as he tried to control his trembling hand, there was no mention of the Bureau of Rectification.

So he dialled information, thinking that an operator would surely be able to find it, but a computerized voice told him that there was no such listing.

Professor Withers looked at his watch. It was now twelve-thirty. He had exactly two and a half hours. With so little time left, he decided that the only thing to do was to take the subway to the government district and search for the mysterious bureau on foot.

So Professor Withers hurried out of his office and

hopped onto a downtown train, wondering what the consequences would be if he failed again to arrive on time.

CHAPTER 9

When Professor Withers reached the government district, he wandered, frightened and bewildered, like a child who had lost his way. Huge columns rose up forbiddingly before him as he made his way through the maze of deserted streets; strange-looking gargoyles beckoned him from the top of their lopsided arches. Dazed, he roamed the narrow pathways that snaked through the massive stone facades and weaved in and out of winding alleys and crooked lanes. Passing through empty plazas—abandoned courtyards that were more intimidating than inviting—he wondered why not a soul was to be seen. As he strayed, stooped and dejected, he felt like a foreigner in a strange land, like a man trapped in a bizarre dream. The oppressive architecture weighed him down, the stark atmosphere filled him with dread as he searched futilely, ending up, it seemed, in the same place again and again.

Finally, after what seemed an eternity, he stumbled upon a strange little man, huddled by a fire on an abandoned street corner.

"Keep going that way," the man said, before Professor Withers had had a chance to speak. "Until you come to a crook in the road. You can't miss it."

"That way?" Professor Withers said.

"Yes," the man said, pointing in the opposite direction. "That way. You can't miss it," he repeated as he vanished in the blinding snow.

Professor Withers crossed the street and followed the narrow pathway as far back as it went, stumbling at last upon a building which was dwarfed by its towering neighbours. It was constructed of heavy, gray stone and above its portal were curious-looking letters which were obscured in frost and snow.

Gripping the icy railing, Professor Withers climbed the stone steps that led to the entrance and entered a cavernous chamber. He wandered through the dark foyer until he noticed, at the far end, beneath a massive chandelier, a small black counter above which was hung a neon sign that read "Start Here."

Professor Withers' footsteps echoed against the hard, marble floor as he made his way to a small desk which was occupied by a young man, whose tiny frame appeared diminished against the immensity of the hallway.

"May I help you?" the young man asked, rising from his chair.

"Yes," he answered. "I have an appointment with the Bureau of Rectification."

"Bureau of Rectification?"

"Yes," Professor Withers responded. "I've been looking for it all afternoon."

The young man sat down again and searched through his database, his fingers magically dancing across the keyboard. Then he stood up and grimaced, letting out a howl that echoed through the empty chamber.

'There is no Bureau of Rectification, Professor Withers."

"But—."

Professor Withers leaned against the marble counter for support.

"They came to visit me," he began.

His body started to tremble, and his face became drawn in anguish.

"They told me to show up today. Where am I supposed to go? Why don't they tell me?"

"Just keep looking," the clerk responded, sitting down, smiling again, his voice gentle and soothing. "You're bound to find it. Would you like me to call you a cab?"

"No. Thank you. I don't think I'll need a cab."

Professor Withers followed his footprints back through the long, endless chamber, obscured by the darkness that enveloped the room, until he came to the exit.

"Sir," the young man said, appearing out of nowhere.

"Your cab is here."

The young man tipped his hat and opened the door. "You don't want to miss your appointment."

CHAPTER 10

Early that evening, Professor Withers arrived back at his apartment. Trembling and exhausted, he kicked off his shoes and fell back into his aging armchair. He tried to rest. He tried to forget everything that was happening to him. He tried to convince himself that he was not the least concerned about the two inspectors. He had, he reasoned, done nothing wrong and, therefore, had nothing to fear. After all, *he* was the victim. It was his right to proceed with the investigation if he chose to. And, when all was said and done, if he were ever questioned, he knew he could say, in all honesty, that he had done his best to find the enigmatic Bureau of Rectification.

But the events of the day kept looming before him like a tenacious nightmare that refused to loosen its grip: the Dean, his head dangling before him on a tightly wound spring; Miss Watkins, hovering like a voodoo doll, mutating from a snake into a vulture and back, slithering through his mind until he could no longer bear the image. And then there was the young man at the bureau: grimacing like a demon, then announcing the arrival of a cab he had never requested.

Just when he thought he would go mad, the phone started to ring, jolting him back to reality. He stared at the device, frightened, yet determined, as it rang repeatedly, to ignore its incessant sound, attempting to convince himself that it was nothing more than a prank call. He tried everything to avoid answering. He fixed himself dinner. He reviewed the mound of mail that had accumulated in his mailbox. He flipped through old magazines he had not noticed or had not had the time to read, doing his best to ignore the sinister ringing that refused to cease. At last, unable any longer to bear it, he picked up the receiver and placed it against his ear.

"You missed your appointment again, Professor Withers," came the voice on the other end. "I warned you of the consequences."

Professor Withers considered for a moment whether to respond, weighed, for the first time since this ordeal had begun, how to react and what tone of voice to use should he choose to answer.

At last, in a voice he could not control, he said: "Where am I supposed to go?"

"That's not for us to say."

"I don't understand," Professor Withers said, losing his patience. "You want me to assist you in investigating a crime in which *I* was the victim and this is the way you behave? How do I know you're for real?"

"What would you say, Professor Withers, if I told you that I know everything you do? Every move? Every word you say? Your trip to the government quarter today, for example. Your visit to the Office of Miscellaneous Affairs."

"Who are you?" Professor Withers said, growing impatient.

"You will know in due time, Professor Withers. For now, let us just say that it's in your best interest to meet with us. You *will* meet with us, Professor Withers, whether you want to or not."

Professor Withers considered Agent LeFabvre's words. He did not want to respond but he knew that no response was a response, in and of itself. Yet, responding, it seemed, would lead to the same cycle of events which had already led him to nowhere.

"And if I don't?" he said at last.

"You *will* meet with us, Professor Withers. Don't you understand? You have no choice in the matter."

"Where? Where am I supposed to go?"

"You will know. Just continue as you have and you will find me."

"But—."

"That's all there is to it. You see how easy? Tomorrow, shall we say—one o'clock?"

With a hollow click, the phone went dead, and

Professor Withers stared into the receiver as if he expected it to reconnect, then placed it back on the hook and stared into space.

CHAPTER 11

That night, the spectre of Agent LeFabvre haunted Professor Withers like a relentless apparition, threatening him with horrid, untold consequences, looming before him like a determined demon that refused to release its unholy grip. Professor Withers tossed and turned, awoke and dozed, slipping into short bouts of restless sleep from which he would fitfully stir, confused and shaken, before sinking back again into a murky stupor, until, as the long, turbulent night at last came to an end, he could barely distinguish the difference between dream and reality.

At the crack of dawn, as the sun dissolved the dark demons into a soft haze of soothing light, he decided to return to the office he had visited the day before. Perhaps the young man at the information desk would be able to help. Perhaps someone there would know how to direct him.

At nine o'clock, Professor Withers boarded an empty subway car and headed for the government quarter, winding his way once again through the empty streets, searching for the bureau he had visited just the day before. He proceeded warily along the slushy sidewalks, manoeuvred around fresh mounds of snow, trudged through unshovelled pathways that led him to endless back alleys and hidden side streets.

At last, shivering in his overcoat, he came to the small, indistinct structure, deep in the heart of the district, its dilapidated steps not yet cleared, its name hidden beneath thick piles of white snow, as mysterious and indistinguishable as when he had first seen it. Grasping the iron railing for support, he climbed the steep, icy steps and entered through a heavy, metal door where a sudden rush of hot air seized him. Professor Withers made his way through the empty lobby to the information desk where, instead of the young clerk who had greeted him the day before, a short spectre of a man now sat and eyed him suspiciously from behind a pair of wiry glasses.

"You'll have to go to the reference officer," the man said, before Professor Withers had had a chance to speak.

The man looked straight at him, as his words echoed through the vast lobby, his face stiff and unwelcoming, his voice as mechanical and flat as if he had uttered the same sentence thousands of times.

"Go down the hall, take the elevator to the third floor, make a right. Thirteenth door on your left."

Professor Withers boarded the old, wooden elevator, whose metal gates grated as they opened and closed, and waited in silence. As it made its way up, a heavy smell of oil emanated from its ancient core and permeated the thick, stale air.

Exiting on the third floor, he followed the long, dark corridor and counted the unmarked doors until he came to the specified bureau. After knocking tentatively on the massive portal, he waited a moment, then turned the squeaky doorknob and entered.

It was a large room, poorly lit for its size, with huge, iron fixtures hung from the high ceiling and frosted glass globes that had become yellowed over time and were speckled with the black corpses of insects. The dark, wooden walls seemed to absorb what little light the massive lamps provided, leaving the rest of the chamber flooded in shadow. In the centre of the room were several long wooden benches which made Professor Withers feel like he had just entered a church. He wondered, as he looked around, whether the stuffy, airless atmosphere was intentional, meant to calm the nerves of distraught citizens before presenting their cases, or whether it was simply due to time and neglect, a reflection of an era when government bureaus were designed to appear weighty and ponderous.

At the head of the room was a sign that read: "Fill out a request form, take a number and have a seat."

Professor Withers walked over to the small, wooden

table beneath the sign, peeled off a form and set about filling it out. When he was finished, he folded it in two, as indicated, deposited it in the slot on the wall, and withdrew a number from the metal dispenser on the table.

"99," he read before looking up at the electronic sign, which announced that number 65 was being served, and he turned his number this way and that to make sure he had not misread.

Professor Withers took a seat and waited in silence, expecting other petitioners like himself to come in or at least a clerk with whom he could make inquiries, but the room remained empty and silent, as if its existence were unknown.

Just as Professor Withers was beginning to give up hope, the door at the front of the room swung open, and a spindly little man with a thinning pate of white hair and a pair of thick, round glasses appeared.

"Jeremy Randolph Withers," he called out in a loud voice, clearing his throat and repeating himself once again.

Professor Withers rose from his chair.

"Which of you is Jeremy Randolph Withers?" the man asked, eyeing him suspiciously from the tip of his pointed nose.

"I am," Professor Withers said.

"Then you need to state so clearly. This isn't some kind of guessing game, you know. There's lots of work to be done. Well, come along then. I haven't got all day, you know. I'm a very busy man. Lots of files to review. Lots of cases to settle. Let's not dilly-dally."

The little man spun on his heels, threw the door open, and proceeded down a long, narrow hallway.

"My name is Mr. Fontaine," he said. "I'll be your case officer. You'll tell me everything about your case. I'll then look into the matter and get back to you. The process takes several weeks, sometimes more, sometimes less, depending on the season and the nature of the situation."

"Excuse me," Professor Withers said. "I've just come to ask—"

Mr. Fontaine stopped and turned around.

"I'll do the asking around here," he said, shoving his round, little face up into Professor Withers' nose. "Is that understood?"

"Yes," Professor Withers replied.

"Not a word, not a word. Now, please step into my office and have a seat."

Professor Withers followed him into a small, windowless room and sat down as directed. The strange little man settled himself behind his minuscule desk, removed his glasses, rubbed his eyes, then placed the frames back on his face before beginning.

"Now," he said, clearing his throat and taking a close look at the empty file before him, "what can I do for you, Professor Jeremy Randolph Withers?"

"I'm looking for the Bureau of Rectification," Professor Withers began.

"The Bureau of Rectification? This is not the Bureau of Rectification, Professor Withers. If you want a different office, why do you come here wasting my time?"

"If I may explain."

"Yes. Please do. Start from the beginning. I like things clear and chronological so I can register them properly."

Mr. Fontaine picked up a thin, black pen and readied himself for Professor Withers' story.

"I was visited the other day by a man from the Bureau of Rectification."

"And what was this man's name?"

"Agent Simon LeFabvre. And his assistant, Agent John Smith."

"You said one man. Was there one man or were there two? Please let's get the facts straight here. Clarity, clarity. I must record this accurately and logically."

"There were two men. They came to see me to investigate a crime."

"A crime? And what was this crime?"

"I was attacked in the subway by a youth gang."

"Professor Withers. I asked you to start from the beginning. Is this crime the beginning of your story?"

"Yes, I think so."

"You *think* so? Professor Withers, you are confusing

me, and that is not in your best interest if you want me to proceed with your case."

"That's when it all began. But there were other events that preceded it and seem to be related, though I'm only now beginning to recognize that. Do you understand?"

"No, I don't," Mr. Fontaine responded with an exasperated look on his face. "And I don't understand why everyone who comes here has the same problem. But please proceed. Perhaps it will all become clear."

"Well, then I went to see the Dean and he told me I had missed two weeks of class and that I had not given my students their final exams. But I know I did, because I've been trying to correct them now for three days, only I keep getting interrupted by Agent LeFabvre, who insists that I find him, and the Dean, who insists that I have not done my job."

"I see," Mr. Fontaine said, though his face was clearly flush with confusion. "Is there anything else I need to know?"

Professor Withers thought for a moment, recalling everything that had happened to him over the last couple of days.

"Yes," he said at last. "There's one more thing. My next door neighbour."

"Yes. Your next door neighbour. And what is your neighbour's name?"

"Mrs. Brown. Mrs. Iris Brown."

"I-ris Brown," Mr. Fontaine repeated as he wrote in his notebook. "Yes, Professor Withers. Please continue."

"Well. She saw me that day—"

"And which day was that?"

"The day this all began. December fourth. She told me that I was dead."

"Dead? Just like that? She just said you were dead."

"At first I thought she hadn't recognized me. But when I told her who I was, she said I was dead."

"I see. This is a very serious situation, Professor Withers. Are you dead or not? Do you have a death certificate?"

"No. I don't."

"Well then you can't be dead, can you?" Mr. Fontaine shouted in an exasperated voice. "Everyone who dies must be issued a death certificate. It's the law. So you're either not dead or you're breaking the law. Now which is it?"

Professor Withers reached into his pocket for his handkerchief and began patting the sweat that had appeared on his brow as his hands trembled from the strain.

"Professor Withers, this is a very serious situation. A woman makes a claim that you are dead. A man declares that you haven't shown up to work for two weeks. It's a good thing you came here today. This is something that must be investigated."

"But what about Agent LeFabvre?" Professor Withers said. "How do I find him?"

"That is not my concern at the moment. If you want to find him, you'll have to go through the proper channels."

"But that's what—"

"Professor Withers—"

"—I came here for today."

"Professor Withers—"

"It's my right. I demand to see him. I demand to have this entire situation resolved so I can get on with my life."

"Professor Withers!" Mr. Fontaine shouted. "You must listen to me. I'm a very busy man. I don't have time to waste. You have come here for my help, and I will help you if you allow me to. Now will you listen?"

"Yes," Professor Withers said. "I'm sorry."

"Now you report that you are dead, yet you don't have a death certificate. And you report that you are seeking a Mr. Simon LeFabvre, yet you don't know who he is or where his office is located. These are all very serious matters. I will look into them for you. But for your own sake and for the sake of those around you, I must advise you to go back home and stay there until you hear from me. Do not leave your house except for urgent matters."

"But I have to find him—"

"I repeat. Do not leave your house except for urgent

matters, Professor Withers. I cannot have a dead man roaming the streets freely without proper documentation. Now, is that understood?"

"Yes. But—"

"But? There are no buts when things are understood. Good day, then."

CHAPTER 12

Late that afternoon, as he rode through the depths of the city on an ancient subway car that creaked and groaned and crawled along tracks that had been laid more than a century before, Professor Withers wondered how else to proceed. He had tried, in earnest, to find Agent LeFabvre. Now he was faced with yet another quandary in which he was becoming further mired: another government bureau which had grabbed him with its tentacles and refused to let him go. Every step he took led to a maze of setbacks from which there seemed no return. Every attempt to perform what should have been a simple procedure—filing a crime report—took him deeper and deeper into a quagmire, a black hole from which there was no escape.

His hands were trembling. He held them up in desperation: flabby, wrinkled hands that, under the harsh light of the subway car, seemed barely alive. He stared at them, terrified, exerted every effort to stop them from shaking.

Frustrated, he dug his hands into the frayed, straw-like upholstery, into the old cotton insides which were dry and warm, soothing and tranquilizing. For a moment, he thought he saw the young man from the information desk sitting beside him, but then the harsh sound of the subway car rushing through the darkness broke the spell, intruded on this brief flash of calm, until the young man disappeared into a crowd of lifeless straphangers.

When the packed train finally came to his stop, Professor Withers slipped through the crowd of motionless travellers, each frozen in time and space, and walked through the deserted station. How many times had he gone through this motion? he wondered. Hundreds, even thousands. An action that had become incorporated into his life, one and inseparable, like the motion of a bee who comes and goes from the same flower because his life depends on it. Yet now, for the first time, he noticed how old and dirty the station was. He examined the cracked, discoloured tiles, the filthy platform caked with the grime of generations, the ancient, graffiti-filled columns that rose from the worn gray concrete up to the ceiling, pocked with old paint that flaked with the disease of age. In all the years he had ridden the subway, it seemed as if it had never once been repaired or refurbished. If the government, he thought, was so unconcerned about a system so vital to the city's survival, how much effort would they put into resolving the case of one insignificant, old man? How long, he wondered, climbing the grimy, broken steps that led to the outside world, would it be before his situation, which became more and more complicated as time went by—how long would it be before the authorities would be able to untangle it?

He would obey Mr. Fontaine's request, for now, he decided as the fresh air hit him with the force of reason. He would stay in his apartment, wait for the strange little clerk to contact him, wait for Agent LeFabvre who would surely call. He had no choice, it seemed. Not at this time of his life. He would sit and wait. What else could he do?

Professor Withers stopped at the grocery store. He bought vegetables, fruits, bread, eggs, canned foods, milk—enough of each to last for a week. It was a reasonable supply, he thought. Any more and things would spoil. Any less and he would certainly be forced to go against the instructions he had been given by Mr. Fontaine. And he knew he could not expect things to proceed in less time than that.

And if the week passed and he had still not heard from Mr. Fontaine—? Well, he would worry about that when the time came.

CHAPTER 13

The evening passed uneventfully, though Professor Withers sat on edge, in his aging armchair, waiting for something new and dreadful to occur. He had come to expect the unexpected, had begun to accept its presence in his life, like a cancer victim succumbs to the fact that each day may bring further regression. Anticipating some sinister event to jar him out of this strange interval of tranquillity, he flipped through books and magazines the entire evening, his eyes drawn to the telephone which he fully expected would jolt him out of complacency.

By the end of the night, when it was time for him to retire, he made his usual rounds through the apartment to check that everything was as it should be—the lights out, the coffee maker off, the door to his unit double locked—and found himself so unnerved by the uneventfulness of the evening that he began to feel a bit out of sorts. Still, he put his head down on his pillow and, after checking several times to make sure the telephone was indeed on the hook—why hadn't Agent LeFabvre called him, he wondered, feeling distressed without fully knowing why—fell asleep.

The next morning, though he had nowhere to go, he woke up at six. He was an early riser, something that had been instilled in him as a child, and though he had no need for an alarm clock, he always set it knowing full well he would awake the next day without it.

Professor Withers rose as usual from his bed, performed his regular morning rituals, and dressed, as he always did, in a pair of navy blue slacks and a brown Oxford jacket with his shirt opened just at the collar, as if he were going to the university to attend to his duties.

Satisfied, he sat down at the kitchen table and had his usual cup of black coffee, a slice of whole wheat toast and one boiled egg, not too hard, yet not so loose as to require the use of a spoon.

When breakfast was over, when his daily morning routine had come to an end, he settled himself in the living room, taking a seat in the old threadbare armchair beside the window that looked out onto the courtyard in the middle of the complex and found himself, for the first time in his life, with nothing to do. It was a frightening predicament, he thought, one for which he had no preparation.

He sat, stared out the window and wondered how to fill up his time— wondered just how long this stretch of stillness would last. He wished he had not forgotten his students' exams in his office. He glanced around the apartment, noticed, for the first time, things he had never paid attention to—the photograph of his mother on the mantel, stern and dour despite her feeble attempt at a smile; his university diploma dangling on the wall, centred above the fireplace, yellowed and dusty, having been neglected, like everything else, for all these years; and, on the other side, a black and white photograph of himself, set there by his mother to balance the composition, as if to remind him, in life and in death, of his inextricable ties to her. It had been taken on the morning he left to begin his career at the university. He had been only twenty-six at the time and donned a new suit and a perfectly ironed shirt. In his hand, he held the new briefcase she had given him upon graduation. It was a reward, she had said at the time, for all his hard work, a reminder, too, of the responsibilities that lay ahead of him. He was smiling, wistfully, a young man on the brink of promise.

Professor Withers had a sudden rush of panic. How had he ended up like this? Beyond hope, with nowhere to turn. Here he sat, like a man on his deathbed, like a prisoner in solitary waiting for his sentence. He wanted to break loose. He wanted to escape, but he didn't know how, knew he could not disobey Mr. Fontaine, understood that no matter where he went, the spectre of Agent LeFabvre would most certainly follow him. And so he sat and stared out the window, a long life behind, stared into an eternal gulf of emptiness that presented itself through this lone portal to the outside world.

As if to steady himself, Professor Withers gripped the sides of his chair. For the first time, he became aware of the sound of quiet as the grandfather clock, ticking away tenaciously in the corner beside the fireplace, entered his consciousness like a guest who had overstayed his welcome. It seized him, caught him up in its rhythmic motion as the pendulum swung back and forth. The heavy silence wrapped its invisible arms around him, and his body trembled as he tried to prevent himself from being swallowed up in its ceaseless march towards eternity.

Then, like a death knell, the clock began to chime, slow and mournful like church bells announcing a funeral. He found the hollow sounds strangely soothing, and he closed his eyes and concentrated, let them cast their spell on him. When the clock chimed its last toll, he listened to the final resonance fade into silence, a silence punctuated only by the steady sound of ticking, and a distant echo of laughter which caught his attention and called him back as if from a dream.

Opening his eyes, he turned towards the window, parted the tattered curtains with his fingers and looked below. Fresh snow, pure and unblemished, filled the courtyard. The brightness blinded him, and he cupped his hands around his eyes as he searched for the source of the gentle laughter. Soon, a cloud covered up the sun, diffusing the reflection of the snow, and he was able make out the figure of a child playing in the square.

Professor Withers watched as the little boy built a snow castle, carving out windows and doors. Then, as he began forming little figurines and placing them here and there in the little landscape he had fashioned, the blinding brightness returned, and the child disappeared.

As the laughter faded into nothingness, Professor Withers heard the sound of a key jangling in his door. He quickly closed the curtains and rushed over to the foyer. The door opened, and Mr. Beasley entered solemnly, walking right past him as if he didn't exist, followed by the neighbours whose sombre expressions filled him with grief: Mrs. Brown, sad and grim, hobbling her way across the room; Laura, nervous and frightened, clutching on to her mother's skirt for protection; Mrs. Jacobs, wiping a tear from her eye, keeping a ghostly distance from the rest as she brought up the rear.

"Hello?" Professor Withers called out.

Heedless, they proceeded into the living room— tenants he had spoken to and residents he had barely seen—until the room was nearly full, flush with the hushed cacophony of a church before the service begins.

Mrs. Brown walked over to the mantel and stared at the photographs of Professor Withers and his mother as she began to weep.

"Such a good son," she said, wiping her face with an embroidered handkerchief. "So good to his mother."

Professor Withers looked on in astonishment.

Laura's mother put her arms around her daughter's shoulders.

"Come," she said, in a comforting voice. "Let's find a place to sit."

"Ladies and gentleman," a man in a black suit announced in a deep, resonant voice. "Let us proceed."

"Proceed?" Professor Withers shouted. "Proceed with what?"

"The courts have determined," the man continued, "that since the deceased had no direct descendants, his property should be ceded to the state."

"What!?" Professor Withers said. "What do you mean deceased?"

"However, it has come to our attention that many of you were like relatives. I understand that some of you even helped raise him. Therefore, it has been decided that you may each take a memento to remember him by. I ask that you now choose and leave in as orderly a fashion as possible so that we can dispose of the remainder of his belongings."

A loud murmur buzzed through the room. Then silence followed, as each waited to see who would begin.

"Please," the man said, holding his hand out in invitation.

Slowly, the neighbours circulated through the apartment.

"Are you all blind?" Professor Withers shouted. "I'm alive. Can't you see? Mrs. Brown. You spoke to me the other day. At the gate. Don't you remember?"

Mrs. Brown reached for the two photos above the mantel and gently lifted them off their hooks. She eyed them for a moment, then turned to leave the room.

"Those are mine," Professor Withers shouted.

"Mother," Laura called, holding up an antique camera she had found in the closet. "Look at this! Can we keep it? Please, Mother."

"This is an insult," Professor Withers said. "I thought you were friends!"

The neighbours continued to peruse his belongings, selecting items and then taking their leave as Professor Withers watched in disbelief, his protests ignored, as his possessions were taken right before his weary eyes, as if his existence were a thing of the past.

When all the neighbours were gone, when most of the items he had collected over his life had disappeared, what remained was hauled away, piece by piece, the very objects that, combined, summed up Professor Withers' long and inconsequential life.

Professor Withers complained, tried preventing them from stealing what was his, but he remained powerless against them.

Late that afternoon, he saw his last possession carried away, a small night table where he would place his books and his glasses each night before retiring. What remained was his favourite armchair, which was deemed too beyond repair to be worth anything, the telephone, which would be dealt with by the telephone company, and the bed which the men were unable to remove no matter how they tried.

"God knows how they got it in here," one of them commented.

"Through the window, no doubt," Mr. Beasley said.

"We will make special arrangements to pick up the bed later," the lawyer said. Professor Withers watched in disbelief as the men left his apartment, listened as the apartment manager turned the key in the lock and their voices faded down the hollow hallway.

CHAPTER 14

Professor Withers sat in his old, dusty armchair and stared out the window. He had been sitting like this for several hours now, ever since the door had been locked behind him. Outside his window, the snow fell, lighting up the darkness that had overtaken the city, burying the courtyard in a thick, heavy blanket that absorbed every sound that was made.

Professor Withers waited, though for what, he was not sure. It was too late in the day for Mr. Fontaine to call, too early at any rate since he had said his case would take several weeks. And throughout the entire day, Agent LeFabvre had remained silent, not once phoning him or making any sort of contact.

Perhaps it was all an illusion, he thought. An illusion that one believes is happening when, beyond it, something else is really taking place. Like when one is in a theatre or at a film and the reality of fiction takes over the actuality of one's life. The film would end, he thought. The curtain would come down on the play, the actors disperse, the house lights come on, and he would suddenly find himself in the real world, brought back to the reality of life, the reality of his existence. It was philosophy, after all, just like he taught. Everything was an illusion except as one made of it.

Just then, the phone rang, jolted Professor Withers back to reality, broke into the illusion of his life—the life he was living at that very moment—and forced him to face the very reality he had refused to accept.

Slowly, he picked up the phone, felt its weight, its heft, its physicality, in the grip of his hands, looked at the hard, black plastic casing which housed the electronics that allowed him to communicate, examined the curly black cord that connected it to its base, and placed the receiver firmly against his ear.

"Yes, Agent LeFabvre," he said, knowing full well that the time had come when he could no longer escape the appointment he had to keep.

He sat and listened, listened as he had never done before, placed his entire existence into the act of listening as the words that were transmitted over this man-made device filtered into his entire being. Things had to be rectified. Things would be rectified whether he liked it or not.

"Yes," he said at last. "I understand."

His face relaxed as he hung up the phone, and while he did not smile, he neither frowned nor quaked. He felt calm, calmer than he had ever felt in his life.

Slowly, he stood up, looked around his empty apartment, gathered his coat and scarf, and put on his gloves. Then, glancing down at the floor, he noticed his hat, lying in the corner. He picked it up and examined it, brushed off the dust, then placed it on his head.

The door opened and he left. He walked through the solemn hallway, down the darkened stairwell and out to the vacant street. He trudged through the silent snow, made his way to the subway station, climbed down the worn stairs, passed through the turnstile and boarded the empty train that sat waiting for him. The doors closed as he took his seat, and the train pulled away, picked up speed and disappeared into the long dark tunnel, leaving the train station still and empty.

ACKNOWLEDGEMENTS

The Appointment began sometime ago when I was taking a fiction workshop at The Writer's Center in Bethesda, Maryland. Though the fog of memory has set in, I remember getting some very good feedback from the instructor as well as my fellow students. The story has changed considerably since then but I wish to thank those individuals who are now just a vague memory for their sage suggestions. I also want to thanks those individuals at Vine Leaves Press for believing in this story and for bringing it to life and you, the reader.

VINE LEAVES PRESS

Enjoyed this book?
Go to *vineleavespress.com* to find more.